THE
LATENT LUTHIER

E. ROBERT BROOKS

Also by E. Robert Brooks
Pirouette
Wine Thief
Derailed Gears
The Concours Caper

Publishing Coordinator – Sharon Kizziah-Holmes
Cover Design – Jaycee DeLorenzo

Paperback-Press
an imprint of A & S Publishing
A & S Holmes, Inc.

ISBN -13: 978-1-956806-37-3

DEDICATION

Dean Zelinsky- An iconic and innovative independent American luthier

John Siegle- An exceptional guitar virtuoso and patient teacher. The really talented players make it look deceptively easy!

PROLOGUE

Billie Earl was a legendary session guitarist who had gotten his start in the Memphis Blues scene in the 1960s.

Moving to Nashville, he had been in high demand with local bands and regularly recorded with them.

He often performed at many well-known clubs and bars, but then one day he inexplicably vanished…

Until several years later, when he walked into Betty's Grill one night at 2:00am.

My friend, Jerry Eichhorn, and I were there with several other longtime patrons enjoying late after concert drinks and cheeseburgers.

When Billie had disappeared, for several months there had been widespread speculation around town about what had become of him.

Eventually, the gossip had died down, but Billie's fame persisted.

When he walked into the restaurant that night, one of the diners saw him, and yelled, "That's Billie Earl!", and everyone instantly recognized him.

The manager saw Billie, and we overheard her offer him a burger and a drink on the house, and though they would be closing in an hour, she asked if he would like to play a few songs.

Billie looked uncomfortable and replied that he didn't have a guitar with him.

Jerry chimed in on the conversation and offered to give him one of his to play.

Jerry was a third-generation luthier, or maker of stringed instruments.

The guitar he fetched from his truck exhibited a weathered patina, not from abuse, but due to extensive use over many years of play.

Billie scrutinized the pickups and switches of the unfamiliar "axe" and experimented with them to determine the range of settings.

At the same time, he ran the palm of his left hand rapidly up and down the back of the maple neck several times, testing it for friction.

Plucking the strings, he momentarily frowned encountering the unexpected thickness of a wound G string, which was not conducive to his style of bending notes.

He tried different methods of articulating sound from the instrument, eventually nodding in satisfaction.

When Billie plugged into and turned on an amplifier, his fingers flittered over the strings as they wove an intricate and enticing musical pattern.

His audience were initially enraptured by the compelling tempo.

Then, the quickening cadence abruptly dissipated into a drawn-out melancholy sound with disparate tones…

It was an ethereal and complex creation, that, for no apparent reason, reminded me of a gossamer spider's web shimmering in reflected pale sunlight.

This unexpected vision sent a chill down my spine and seemed to whisper reminders of troubling childhood experiences.

The imaginary web almost imperceptibly undulating in the illusion of a faint breeze…

What was his inspiration for this haunting melody, I wondered?

What tribulations had contributed to this erratic soul-searching style of play?

Perhaps memories of the demise of a cherished

loved one, or a lost muse from his past who had left invisible scars on his heart evoking emotions expressed through musical compositions?

CHAPTER ONE

A mong musicians, historically, the consensus has been that America has the reputation as the preeminent country in the world for designing and producing guitars.

The two most influential manufacturers are Fender and Gibson.

After World War II, Fender, based in California, was credited with designing the lap steel guitar.

They went on to lead solid-body electric guitar design trends with famed models such as the Broadcaster (which became the Telecaster) and the Stratocaster.

However, in early 1965, Fender was sold to a

subsidiary of Columbia Broadcasting Systems, named Columbia Records Distribution Corporation.

In the opinion of many of the Fender employees, under the new ownership quality diminished and innovation stagnated.

Gibson is a much older company than Fender, commencing operations in Kalamazoo, Michigan in 1894.

Their initial reputation came from their acoustic guitars and mandolins, which were patterned after the archtop design of the violin.

As with Fender, over time, the ownership of Gibson changed.

In 1944, Chicago Musical Instrument Company (CMI) acquired Gibson.

In 1969, CMI merged with an Ecuadoran brewery, called FCL, and the new parent company of Gibson was renamed as Norlin.

In 1974, Gibson expanded production and opened a second factory in Nashville, Tennessee.

In 1983, Norlin was sold to Piezo Electric Products, and the new owners shut down the Kalamazoo operation, made the Nashville facility the headquarters, and eventually divested of the music division.

In 1986, the new owners of Gibson attempted to restore the brands solvency and reputation.

For several years, they were successful with

reinvigorating the company by introducing new designs, sponsoring popular artists, and increasing their advertising.

However, they subsequently suffered a significant financial reversal when due to a malicious political grudge, the Obama administration falsely accused them of using illegally imported wood species in the construction of their guitars.

Nevertheless, in the mid-1970s business was brisk for Gibson, and the future looked bright…

CHAPTER TWO

J erry Eichhorn's grandfather, Ernst, who made violins, violas, and zithers, had learned his craft from master European luthiers through the time-honored apprentice system.

In the 1930s, his family lived in what became East Germany after World War II.

Jerry's grandfather was too old to relocate prior to the outset of hostilities with the invasion of nearby Poland, despite believing the growing fascist political climate in his country was alarming and detrimental.

But Ernst worried about the younger members of his family.

Before war was declared, he scraped together enough money to send them to America on a tramp steamer in the steerage section.

They eventually arrived in New York and made their way to the Midwest where they settled in Michigan.

Though Germans were not welcome in many parts of America in those days, Jerry's father was a trained artisan with useful skills.

He went to work for Gibson in Kalamazoo, Michigan, where he specialized in constructing hollow body acoustic guitars.

Gibson management did not share the prevalent anti-German sentiment of the time.

They hired and worked with several German craftsmen, including Les Paul, who was also of Prussian extraction, and had been born in Waukesha, Wisconsin as Lester Polsfuss.

After the war, when Jerry was old enough, he went to work for Gibson too and assisted his father.

Jerry eventually became an accomplished luthier in his own right.

He moved to Nashville when Gibson opened their facility there.

He initially settled in the suburb of Germantown, where many families shared his heritage, and he was welcomed.

Ultimately, he came to feel that the increasingly

corporate environment at Gibson was becoming too restrictive.

He moved out of the city to Kingston Springs and struck out on his own as an independent maker of custom guitars.

The Nashville area was an exciting place to be involved in the music scene in the 1970s.

Recognized as the capital of Country Music, and a hotbed of talent for Blues and Jazz (although Bristol was the actual birthplace of Country Music, and Memphis was also a significant scene for Blues, early Rock and Roll, R&B, and Soul Music), Nashville provided many opportunities for Jerry to form friendships with influential artists who featured and promoted his guitars.

CHAPTER THREE

Jerry always carefully combined dissimilar woods to construct the bodies of his guitars, with different densities and sonic characteristics.

He eschewed using popular exotic species such as Rosewood, Koa, Cocobolo, Ebony and Korina, and instead harvested his own indigenous hardwoods.

He most often chose black walnut, and swamp ash which was abundant prior to the Emerald Ash Borer invasion twenty-five years later.

He felt these varieties were structurally strong and stable with complimentary tones, and the difference in coloration was visually striking.

For the neck construction, rock maple with a flame pattern was his preferred choice, complimented by stainless steel frets.

Though these choices were difficult to cut and shape, they were robust and resistant to wear and warping.

His priority was to determine the voice of the guitar, the cumulative sound which was the result of carefully inspecting and considering all the influences of the individual components.

When he combined these materials and techniques with the proprietary construction methods handed down to him by his father, the result was a unique sound with a vibrant sustain that had become a signature characteristic of his guitars.

However, the overall visual impression was also important to showcase the aesthetics of his style.

He used only the finest materials, including high quality metals and electronics, and he laboriously hand wound the copper wire for his custom pickups.

His designs featured intricate bindings and inlays that displayed ancient druidic symbols.

Most notably, the flowing spirit of Awen, which was expressed by three rays of light.

Through the ages, this image was considered a symbol of inspiration and divine illumination for poets, writers, and artists.

Perhaps, because of this association with Celtic

imagery, some musicians who played his guitars attributed mystical powers to their instruments.

Jerry prided himself on paying painstaking attention to all the small details, such as the elegantly machined knurling on the potentiometers, as well as the deep luster and durability of the wood finishes, which all contributed to a players visual and tactile impressions.

He was well-aware that having a beautiful and unique instrument to appreciate and show off to an admiring audience provided some of his customers with added pride and confidence during their performances.

As he hiked through the forest at the back of his property to examine mature timber for suitability, he discerned individual trees with interesting shapes that almost seemed to silently call out to him, and draw him to them…

Their lofty heights and the girth of their trunks were physical manifestations of the passage of time.

Once felled and rough cut, he would carefully air dry the wood for a year, or more, rather than resorting to the expedience of kiln-drying, which he felt compromised structural integrity and resonance.

When sufficiently seasoned, he would choose select slabs to construct his instruments, free from knots and cracks, and with highly figured grain patterns.

As he wandered from tree-to-tree, marking the

ones he selected for cutting with orange plastic webbing, he came upon a small ravine.

He slid down the muddy bank, and as he traversed across the bottom to a cleared area, to his horror he saw propped up against the incline on the far side, a partially decomposed human body...

The limbs were akimbo, as if the torso had been mercilessly hurled against the unforgiving ground.

At this distance, the remaining facial features were dirty and obscured, but they looked vaguely familiar...

Hanging by a strap from the neck of the deceased was a broken guitar, that even from afar, by its unique shape he recognized was one of his designs...

CHAPTER FOUR

T he original members of famed Southern Rock band - The Allman Brothers - grew up in Florida.

To further their careers in the music business and take advantage of the opportunity for a recording deal with newly formed Capricorn Records, they moved to Macon, Georgia in 1969.

However, despite considerable success, due to internal dissent the band broke up in 1976 because of the arrest and criminal conviction of their de-facto manager - John "Scooter" Herring, for drug distribution charges.

Against the wishes of his bandmates, the band's leader, Gregg Allman, who was a heroin and cocaine addict, made a deal with the government to testify against Herring in exchange for receiving immunity from prosecution.

Though the Federal Bureau of Investigation (FBI) and the United States Drug Enforcement Administration (DEA) felt they already had an airtight case against Herring, they wanted to really *seal the deal*, and create publicity by using Allman as the insider "star" witness at the trial.

When word got out that Greg Allman had agreed to testify, John "J.C." Hawkins, who was the acknowledged boss of the Georgia branch of the Dixie Mafia, issued a contract on him.

The prosecutor's office put Allman into protective custody to prevent his murder.

Before he became Greg Allman's bodyguard and the tour manager for the band, as well as, their preferred supplier of illegal drugs, Herring had been the driver and right-hand man for Hawkins.

Herring's Dixie Mafia *partner-in-crime*, who was also arrested, was a licensed pharmacist named Joey Fuchs, who provided him with large quantities of cocaine, heroin, Demerol, and other addictive drugs.

CHAPTER FIVE

D ewey "Icepick" Hartley was an enforcer and longtime member of the Dixie Mafia crew out of Biloxi, Mississippi.

He had done five years hard time at the Angola State Penitentiary after getting caught robbing a warehouse in Louisiana, by cops who weren't on the take, a rarity in those days.

Since his release, as a front for selling stolen parts and laundering money, he had been running a small motorcycle repair shop for his gang in Macon, Georgia, where "Scooter" Herring, who rode with him, had worked as a mechanic.

On the day Herring was arrested by the FBI at the Allman Brothers Band office and Fuchs was apprehended at his home, Hartley was at the motorcycle shop and narrowly avoided the same fate.

When he heard the news by phone from an informant in the Sheriff's office of the impending arrests, he quickly packed up his few possessions, turned off the lights for the last time, locked the garage and front doors, and hit the road.

His plan was to head north to Tennessee and join back up with his former Hillbilly Mob compatriot, William "Blue Eyes" Miller.

Miller was a notorious cold-blooded contract killer who had recently moved to Nashville to avoid possible incarceration, and to take over the gang's business interests in the state in the aftermath of the murders of three of their members in the early 1970s.

Tennessee Sherriff Buford Pusser had allegedly assassinated them as vengeance for an attempt on his life, and for the killing of his wife, Pauline, in retaliation for his crackdown on Dixie Mafia activities in the area.

Though Kirksey McCord Nix, Jr., who was rumored to have been the ringleader of the plot to murder Pusser and his wife, evaded Pusser's wrath, he was subsequently convicted in 1972 of murdering a New Orleans grocery executive.

He was sentenced to life without parole at Angola prison, where he met Hartley, who was also serving time there.

Icepick was riding a Harley-Davidson Duo-Glide model with a Panhead motor that sported custom fish tail mufflers, instead of the more common fish mouth design, and a shiny chrome skull prominently mounted on the front fender.

He had forcibly taken the bike from a bartender who was behind on gambling and prostitution debts.

It was a heavy machine and didn't have the style or performance of the flashier Sportster models.

Like most older Harleys, even after Herring had rebuilt the motor for him, it still leaked a little oil.

However, it was comfortable for long road trips, and with the large saddlebags it provided adequate storage for his clothing and weapons.

Despite the decorative embellishments, when it came to his machinery, he considered himself a practical man.

No high-rise, ape-hanger handlebars, that were showy, but compromised handling.

Parts like those were for "poseurs," as his Cajun cellmate from the Louisiana Penitentiary used to say!

He thought of himself as a Harley purist, and in his opinion the old school approach of a true kickstart model was the only dependable way to go.

Despite all the Jap bikes equipped with them, he didn't like and was sceptic of the newer Electra-Glides that featured an unreliable electric start, even though the Shovelhead motor design produced more power.

He especially didn't like that the Harley-Davidson worker/owners had sold out to corporate giant AMF, the hated American Machine and Foundry Company!

Ever since they had taken over this legendary American brand, quality and innovation had suffered, and the bikes were now marketed with glossy magazine ads to middle-aged suburbanites!

CHAPTER SIX

T he music business in 1970s America was run by ruthless corporations specializing in convincing and compelling up-and-coming musicians to sign away their rights.

Onerous contracts were very profitable for the companies, but generally left the artists with meager compensation.

For the talent agents who represented the musicians, successfully promoting a record often required providing drugs, sexual favors, and extensive bribes to record company executives and club owners.

In those days, the Italian Mafia ruled many of the big cities and was heavily involved in the music business.

In the 1970s, there were approximately six thousand radio stations in America.

At least four thousand were reputed to have pay-to-playlists under Cosa Nostra control.

The Dixie Mafia, otherwise known as The Hillbilly Mob, operated throughout the Gulf Coast, and was not as well-known as the Sicilian Mafia.

Though not directly connected with the Italians, the Dixie Mafia worked with them on occasion, carrying out contract killings and collecting money for them when it was advantageous and profitable to do so.

The membership of the Dixie Mafia was often drawn from prisons where hardened criminals were recruited.

They initially gained notoriety running illegal booze and expanded into all manner of related criminal activities, including extortion, gambling, prostitution, rigging elections, and murder for hire.

Members of the gang routinely coerced and corrupted law enforcement and public officials with bribes, blackmail, and threats.

Though Prohibition in America ended in 1933, many states and counties in the South remained dry into the 1950s and 1960s.

As laws changed and bootlegging was no longer profitable, they expanded into illegal drug distribution.

While the Italian Mafia was initially reticent to enter the drug trade, several years later they followed suit.

"Anything for a buck," was the Dixie Mafia mantra, and they plied their destructive wares without compunction.

These days, Las Vegas is known as Sin City, but in the 1950s, Phenix City in Alabama bore the moniker, and it was the home base for the Dixie Mafia.

The situation there became so dangerous, that the Governor of Alabama declared martial law and brought in a decorated World War II general to end the corruption and restore law and order.

In response, the criminals moved across the state line into Mississippi and set up their new headquarters in Biloxi.

Mike Gillich, Jr. was the Dixie Mafia's anointed kingpin and ran his operations out of Biloxi, in an area known as "The Strip," where he owned commercial real estate and controlled many of the illegal enterprises.

He was the compatriot of Kirksey McCord Nix, Jr., who was the son of a prominent Oklahoman judge, and one of the gang's most notorious hitmen.

Nix was a lieutenant for Darrel Ward, who controlled Dixie Mafia operations out of Clarksville, Texas, and was the gang's primary liaison with notorious Chicago Mob boss Sam Giancana.

CHAPTER SEVEN

The eastern portion of Tennessee, in the Appalachian Mountains, has a long history of making artisanal distilled spirits.

Immigrant Scots and Irish used local corn to make potent clear unaged whiskey, which became colloquially known as "white lightning."

Contrary to urban legend, the "XXX" on a jug does not signify that the contents are lethal (although they can be).

This marking by the distiller indicates that the whiskey has been rectified (run through the still) three times and is pure alcohol.

When the American government first tried to tax

these homemade concoctions, they met with stiff resistance.

Moonshiners (so named because they located their stills in remote wooded areas and secretly made their hooch late at night, illuminated by moonlight), conspired with bootleggers (a term coined in the 1880s which referred to hiding flasks of liquor in their boot tops), who smuggled the liquor to avoid the taxes.

This illicit activity resulted in antipathy and armed conflict with deputies from the United States Marshals Service and Internal Revenue Agents (irreverently called revenuers).

When prohibition was enacted in Tennessee in 1920, the black-market trade in making and bootlegging whiskey expanded.

Ingenious backyard mechanics came up with methods to modify their cars to hide the contraband.

They "souped-up" their engines so they could outrun pursuing law enforcement.

Many of these outlaws practiced and refined their driving skills with impromptu illegal road races against each other.

Over time, some of them segued into competing professionally in the new sport of stockcar racing, which became NASCAR.

Statewide prohibition in Tennessee was abolished in 1937, but many counties in the state remained "dry" and bootlegging continued.

Even in modern times, though licensed and bonded local distilleries have become famous for their wood-aged corn whiskies, some counties in Tennessee still prohibit off-premise liquor sales by retail stores, and/or on-premise sales in restaurants, hotels, and bars.

When "Icepick" Hartley rolled up into Nashville, there was already a well-entrenched criminal network in the state for him to collaborate with…

CHAPTER EIGHT

Billie Earl was a successful musician but, like many gifted artists, did not handle the pressures of increasing fame well.

Outside of his practices and performances, his life became a high-tension train wreck.

His self-obsessed and irascible personality was exacerbated by alcohol and drug addiction, which increasingly resulted in unpredictable and irrational behavior, including subsequent bouts of suicidal depression.

Constantly in debt to the Dixie Mafia, he increasingly incurred their wrath due to the lateness of his payments.

Missing a rendezvous because he hadn't made a payment, and feared harsh punishment, "Blue Eyes" Miller sent Icepick to track him down.

Miraculously, Billie managed to elude Icepick and hid out for over two years in a secluded abandoned log cabin on the Harpeth River outside of White Bluff near Paint Rock Bluff, where prehistoric petroglyphs adorn the rock face of the cliffs.

He avoided almost all interaction with other people, until he made the mistake of convincing himself that enough time had passed that he would no longer face retribution.

In the aftermath of his most recent alcohol and drug fueled binge, Billie awoke from his self-induced coma, eventually stumbled out of bed, and spent the better part of the morning swearing epithets and uttering an almost non-stop string of invectives and vitriol at his bedraggled cat.

He was bored, lonely, and yearned to hear the therapeutic sounds of live music.

His decision to surreptitiously return to Nashville was his undoing…

While most of the city was closing or already asleep, Billie cautiously entered Betty's Grill.

The sensory experience of up-tempo tunes immediately soothed him, enhanced by his imbibement of some powerful moonshine from the manager's private stash.

Though undeniably talented, Billy Earl wasn't a blisteringly fast gunslinger-style guitarist.

He was an erstwhile poet, raised on the melancholy melodies of the Blues, and preferred to play music that tugged at the heartstrings of his listeners.

He understood how to create the effect of poignant suspense and expectation, without resorting to electronic embellishments, by holding and lingering over home notes at the conclusion of his minor progressions.

When the grill closed for the night, he felt rejuvenated as he headed back to White Bluff with the guitar Jerry Eichhorn had given him.

An hour later, as he exited his truck and went to open the cabin door, he shivered in the cool early morning air.

In the distance, he heard the guttural exhaust rumble of an approaching motorcycle echoing off the surrounding hillsides...

CHAPTER NINE

Icepick had convinced Blue Eyes there was big money to be made running drugs through the music scene in Nashville.

He regaled Miller with stories about the large profits Scooter and Fuchs made for the gang through the Allman Brothers band.

Billie Earl was already an established guitarist, and would be their front man, providing drugs to other musicians in the area who played with him.

But Billie proved to be unreliable and self-destructive, and when he ran out on them, Blue Eyes went ballistic!

Now, Icepick figured the chance to redeem

himself and belatedly cash-in on his scheme had arrived.

As he headed for the hills following Earl's pickup truck, Icepick formulated a plan to get back in Miller's good graces.

When he cornered Billie, he easily chased him down and using his trademark armament, mercilessly stabbed him repeatedly with an icepick, while Billie screamed in abject terror.

Icepick relished this satisfying and effective *up close and personal* method of killing his victims.

He enjoyed looking into the eyes of the people he murdered, and seeing their horror change to disbelief, until the last spark of life was extinguished.

Easy to conceal, his icepick effortlessly penetrated deeply into the body, between ribs and other boney obstructions, and the tiny wounds kept blood spatter to a minimum.

Icepick put the dead body in the back of Billie's pickup truck and drove it over to the outskirts of Jerry Eichhorn's property in Kingston Springs.

He took the guitar from the back seat and smashed it against a tree.

Then he staged the corpse, with the broken guitar dangling from its neck by the strap, in a prominent clearing in the woods where he felt sure Jerry would eventually find it.

He reckoned this would send a clear message to Jerry that he better go-along with an ultimatum to provide introductions to his customers and contacts in the music business, so that Icepick could encourage and supply their drug habits.

CHAPTER TEN

The Cheatham County Sheriff's Office responded to Jerry's emergency call.

A portly deputy arrived in his cruiser and followed Jerry on foot to where the body was situated.

When the officer called for backup, and drew his gun and trained it on Eichhorn, it dawned on Jerry he was the primary suspect.

Unbeknownst to Jerry, the Dixie Mafia had infiltrated law enforcement in several regions of Tennessee.

The officer cross-examining him had previously

been a member of the Memphis Police Department, until he was dismissed for suspicion of selling confiscated stolen property.

He was one of many corrupt lawmen in the state who surreptitiously received regular stipends courtesy of Icepick's boss - William Miller.

After Memphis, the deputy worked as a correctional officer at the Tennessee State Prison near downtown Nashville, where he had met members of Miller's gang.

Eventually, the deputy moved to a job with the Sheriff's Department, arranged by Miller.

The lawman had been instructed to put the fear of God into Jerry, so Icepick could blackmail Eichhorn into storing drugs at his guitar workshop, that would then be sent up to Chicago.

Jerry would also be expected to facilitate local sales from that location.

When another deputy and the coroner arrived, Jerry was taken in handcuffs to the sheriff's headquarters in Ashland City, where he was mercilessly questioned for two hours, before his statement was formally recorded.

He was eventually released on his own recognizance with a dire admonition not to leave the state.

Waiting outside the station for him, Icepick casually introduced himself as a close acquaintance of Billie's, who had been called in to be interviewed about the homicide.

He observed Jerry's lack of a vehicle and offered to give him a ride home on his motorcycle.

Jerry wasn't thrilled about the idea of riding on the back of a stranger's motorcycle, but though he looked a little rough around the edges, Icepick seemed like an affable guy.

His only other option was to call friends with the hope of eventually getting picked up.

Under the circumstances, accepting a ride from Icepick seemed like the only viable choice.

It wasn't until they arrived at his house, and Jerry dismounted the bike, that he noticed the chrome skull on the front fender leering at him...

CHAPTER ELEVEN

Jerry looked up from viewing the skull to see Icepick gazing at him intently with an eerie expression.

He saw his face mirrored in the Ray-Ban aviator sunglasses Icepick was wearing.

Though he felt vaguely disturbed, Jerry made a concentrated effort to keep his expression serene and non-committal.

His strong inclination was for Icepick to depart as soon as possible, but when Icepick asked to use his bathroom, he felt he had to be polite and acquiesce.

Icepick emerged from the bathroom, followed

by an unholy stench.

He grinned with tobacco-stained teeth at Jerry's discomfort, and then irreverently inquired about Jerry's experience at the sheriff's station.

As Jerry started to recount the harrowing details of his interview, Icepick boisterously interrupted him and remarked that he and Billie Earl had been business associates.

A puzzled Jerry asked, "In the music business?"

"No. In the drug distribution business," retorted Icepick, "and you will be his replacement."

As Jerry started to vehemently object, he heard footsteps entering his house.

He looked towards the sound and saw the corpulent deputy darkening his doorway...

CHAPTER TWELVE

With the slash of a smile on his porcine facial features, the deputy held up a clear plastic evidence bag with an evil-looking icepick visible inside it.

As Jerry listened in shocked silence, the crooked lawman taunted, "We got your prints on this shiv.

"We lifted copies when I arrested you.

"Now, be a good ole boy and play ball with us, or you gonna take the fall!"

Icepick chimed in, "When you go visiting your customers, you will be our mule.

"And we'll need you to store a few things for us from time-to-time in your workshop.

"How's that sound?"

Jerry was nonplussed and looked back and forth between them, shaking his head in disbelief.

Icepick continued, "You think it over boy.

"Lucky for you that there's no more death penalty in Tennessee, but it'd be a darn shame for you to spend the rest of your life in prison.

"I'll swing back by in a couple o' days to get you started."

The two criminals had themselves a good laugh as they left Jerry to mull over his predicament…

CHAPTER THIRTEEN

Walter "Walt" Coulter was a burnt-out Vietnam veteran, living on the fringe, who had taken to music to try and soothe the recurring nightmares from his wartime experiences.

He had gone off to fight in an unpopular conflict, for a cause he didn't believe in.

But unlike some of the compatriots from his youth, who became conscientious objectors and draft dodgers, he grudgingly decided to accept his "Volunteer State" patriotic duty, and along with over 160,000 other Tennesseans, he went to war, where he served his country honorably for three tours of duty.

Walt had been an accomplished high school athlete, and by nature was a fast learner.

Once he was boots on the ground, he adapted quickly.

He was intensely loyal to his brothers-in-arms, and he became a fierce and cagey fighter against his insurgent opponents.

He assimilated the dirty tricks of unconventional warfare to survive against an elusive guerilla enemy, who were battle-hardened from years of fighting the French before America officially intervened in 1964.

The South Vietnamese troops, who he liaised with to infiltrate behind enemy lines, gave him the *nom-de-guerre* of – "Le Demon."

After his honorable discharge with a Bronze Star medal for meritorious service in a combat zone, Walt returned home a grizzled veteran, aged beyond his years, to an America he no longer recognized.

Instead of being welcomed back as a hero and appreciated for his service and sacrifice, he was shunned and ostracized.

He became a hermit, living in a tent in the backwoods, but he tenuously clung to sanity with the work he accomplished each day working at Gibson in Nashville.

He was able to segue the skills he developed in Vietnam constructing boobytraps by hand from bamboo and other local materials, into woodworking skills crafting guitars.

The Gibson custom shop, where their top models were constructed, did not became officially recognized and split off from the rest of the company until the mid-1980s, when a new owner took over.

However, in the 1970s, Gibson continued their in-house tradition from the 1920s of making specialty guitars, and Walt was one of the artisans at that time who focused on making artist models for special clients.

Even after working at Gibson for several years, Walt had continued a solitary lifestyle.

He concentrated on his work and rarely conversed or hung out with his fellow craftsmen but became fast friends with Jerry Eichhorn.

He and Jerry shared an interest in music and a history of persecution.

To many people in Tennessee in the mid-1970s, Walt was a physical reminder of America's ignominious recent defeat, a manifestation of a war best forgotten, and they treated him like a pariah.

Jerry had been a young boy when his family arrived in America, but he would always remember the antipathy his family faced due to their German heritage.

When Jerry left Gibson to start his own guitar-making studio, he and Walt kept in touch.

They tentatively agreed that Walt would leave Gibson and join Jerry if the business became a success and could support a partner.

CHAPTER FOURTEEN

Right after Icepick and the dirty deputy left his house, Jerry called me and Walt in a panic.

He tersely explained his dire situation to both of us and asked for our help to combat this criminal assault on his liberty and livelihood.

We all agreed that contacting other law enforcement wasn't prudent.

Jerry was still considered a prime suspect in an active investigation, and we didn't know who we could trust.

We decided to meet at Jerry's house that evening to determine an alternative plan.

When I arrived, Jerry procrastinated discussing his situation, preferring to wait for Walt.

As a distraction, he showed me several of his newest creations, including a mysterious looking ink black guitar festooned with bone white astrological symbols.

Seeing the instrument, I imagined a guitarist garbed in a magician's costume playing it onstage while eerie machine-made smoke wafted around him.

Walt looked disheveled when he arrived, with wild, disarray hair, the beginnings of a patchy beard, and dressed in a worn-out army jacket - the only physical tie he held onto from his military service.

He wordlessly put a jug of his homemade moonshine on the table.

Before any words were spoken between us, we each solemnly took a long swig of the potent elixir.

For reasons that eluded me, Walt always seemed to become more lucid when he was drinking his "mountain dew."

While serving his second tour in Vietnam, Walt's closest buddy had been ambushed and killed by a Viet Cong (Viet Nam Cong San) force.

In response, Walt had volunteered for duty with the ultra-secret Military Assistance Command, Vietnam – Special Operations Group, better known as MACV-SOG.

Sometimes, when we had been drinking together by a roaring fire in the deep of the night, Walt would relate stories of his missions behind enemy lines, which chilled our hearts.

If we were going to take on the Dixie Mafia, and crooked lawmen, Walt was a formidable clandestine soldier to have with us.

CHAPTER FIFTEEN

After a brief discussion, and with some trepidation, we agreed Walt should take the lead on formulating our plans, given his experience with covert operations.

Jerry and I were shocked by the enormity of what Walt proposed, but the dangerous situation Jerry found himself in called for desperate measures.

With some furtive glances between us, we silently nodded from time-to-time in agreement.

In order to circumvent any progression of the plot for Jerry's incarceration, the first target would be the deputy.

The rotund officer and the incriminating evidence would ruthlessly be made to "quietly disappear," so that Icepick would not immediately realize he had a problem.

But first, Walt would arrange a very irritating distraction to preoccupy Icepick, so that he wouldn't impede our scheme for the unscrupulous lawman…

CHAPTER SIXTEEN

After a few inquiries among friends in the music business who we knew were heavily involved in the drug scene, we ascertained that Icepick made rounds to the taverns every Wednesday night to collect protection money for Blue Eyes.

He would often linger at these watering holes, where he drank for free and ogled the girls.

That Wednesday evening, Walt discreetly followed Icepick from bar-to-bar.

When Icepick parked his bike in a dark corner of the parking lot at his fourth stop, Walt parked his rickety pickup truck next to the bike as soon as Icepick went inside.

Walt put a quarter cup of liquid corn sweetener, left over from his most recent moonshine mash ingredients, into the gas tank of Icepick's Harley.

The viscous liquid would assimilate better than using dry granulated sugar, with no telltale powdery residue.

He grabbed the handlebars and rocked the bike back-and-forth a few times to make sure that the additive was thoroughly mixed in the gasoline tank.

Once Icepick drove the bike, and the sugary solution was circulated through the warm motor, it would coat the filters, carburetors, and internal parts.

After the engine cooled and the sugar solidified, the Harley would cease to operate and would require a lengthy and laborious teardown, cleaning, and rebuild to restore it.

CHAPTER SEVENTEEN

The next day, the deputy sheriff stopped by Jerry's property again, unannounced, to check up on him, and to reiterate his threats of arrest and prosecution.

Jerry took the opportunity to suggest the alternative plan the three of us conspirators had formulated and rehearsed, one involving a large cash payout to the crooked lawman in return for the icepick.

When the bent deputy heard the proposed amount, he whistled in astonishment and assured Jerry his loyalty was available to the highest bidder!

Jerry indicated the cash was hidden in a discreet location in Nashville and suggested meeting there late the next night to make the exchange.

The newly closed Neuhoff meat packing plant, situated alongside the Cumberland River in the East Germantown neighborhood of North Nashville, was the place Jerry indicated for their covert meeting.

Jerry assured the officer he knew the area well, since it was located near where he had formerly lived, and that the extensive deserted grounds of the recently abandoned factory would provide complete privacy.

The former correctional officer knew the location from when he had worked at the nearby Tennessee State Prison and agreed to the meet.

When Walt had reconnoitered the factory that morning, he had checked to verify that the electricity, water service, and some of the remaining mechanical equipment were still functioning.

Among the discarded items he found was an electric cattle prod, similar in design to the picanas he had used in Vietnam to torture prisoners.

That afternoon, utilizing skills he had learned during his unconventional warfare training, Walt heavily modified the device to deliver a lethal 250 volts.

Jerry met the crooked cop at the appointed time in the Neuhoff parking lot.

They proceeded to the former slaughtering area in one of the buildings.

Along the side of the room were lockers where employees had stored their work clothes and protective gear when the factory was operational.

As Jerry started to open one of the lockers, he saw that the deputy was watching his every movement with growing unease and suspicion.

But the deputy failed to sense or hear Walt, who snuck up behind him and applied the electric prod to the base of the policeman's neck.

There was a loud crackling sound, and the prod jumped in Walt's hand.

The lawman momentarily tensed *in extremis*, uttered a hair-raising gurgling sound, and then dropped to the killing house floor like a rock.

The smell of newly burnt flesh permeated the air, as the three of us laboriously lifted and impaled the heavy body onto a suspended hook and stripped all the clothing off it.

Walt used a large, purposeful-looking knife, with a serrated spine, to cut the throat and bleed out the carcass.

Crimson blood gushed and spurted from the wound and ran in random rivulets down the body and into the floor drain.

Then, he made a large incision down from the breastbone, gutting the corpse and removing the entrails, which he placed in one of the heavy-duty garbage bags we had brought.

We tried to ignore the foul smell as we dragged the heavy body along the slaughterhouse floor to the adjoining packing area, where the machinery for dismembering cattle and hogs remained.

Using both the saw-edge of the knife, and forcefully chopping down with the sharp side when he encountered bone, Walt proceeded to methodically cut the body into six pieces.

Walt had first worked with a power-operated bandsaw in Vietnam at a Mekong Delta boatyard.

Jerry regularly used the bandsaw in his workshop to cut the blanks for his guitars.

Together, they now used one of the plants large meat-cutting saws, outfitted with a stainless-steel blade, to systematically butcher the corpse into many small pieces.

There had not been time to cool, or freeze the meat, making the pieces unwieldy to cut, and slowing the process.

As Walt and Jerry sliced up the chunks, I placed the remains into the other garbage bags.

Once the grisly task was completed, we thoroughly hosed down the saw and the floor, and unceremoniously dumped the sawn-up remains, the officer's clothing, personal effects, and badge, along with our aprons, boots, and gloves, into the murky, sewage-polluted river.

Then we washed out, crumpled up, and threw the now empty garbage bags into an already overflowing fetid dumpster.

When we departed, I drove behind Jerry and Walt in the deceased deputy's off-duty car.

We ditched it once we were well clear of the city limits in a remote area where it would not be found for some time.

Despite Jerry's and my protests, along with the icepick that he had carefully wiped down, Walt had also taken the trooper's pistol.

CHAPTER EIGHTEEN

Our next task was to eliminate the threat of Icepick seeking revenge.

Once he put two and two together and figured out his motorcycle had been purposely incapacitated around the same time his erstwhile mercenary underling and the incriminating weapon had gone missing, he would likely come knocking on Jerry's door looking for answers.

Since relocating to Nashville, Icepick had taken up the habit of chewing Red Man leaf tobacco, which was locally popular since it was manufactured a couple of hours north of the state line in Owensboro, Kentucky.

When he found out what had caused his

motorcycle to break down, Icepick was livid, spitting a large gob of tobacco on the ground.

After two days of rushed repairs with overtime labor expense, it was now operational.

He was finally back on the road and hell-bent on seeking retribution!

The problem was he had no idea who would be fool enough to tangle with him!

Using a prearranged false name, he left a message at the sheriff's station for the crooked deputy to call him, but so far, he had not received any response.

When he finished eating at his favorite diner that evening, he winked at the waitress and then strutted outside to where he had parked his bike.

With his slicked back hair, mutton chop sideburns, and decked out in a pair of shitkicker boots, Icepick apparently fancied himself the definition of "cool."

But the young waitress probably thought he looked like a pathetic throwback, frozen in time from the previous decade.

As he approached his Harley, to his rage, he saw that both tires were flat.

Upon closer examination, he found small holes in the rubber, that looked like they had been caused by nails, or, it dawned on him, they could have been caused by an icepick…

He fumed about having to call the local motorcycle shop again for a tow and vowed to find the perpetrator and make him suffer!

CHAPTER NINETEEN

The ambush was set along a lonely stretch of backcountry road, about nine miles from Jerry's house.

I was waiting on a bluff overlooking the approach to Jerry's property to alert him and Walt, by walkie-talkie, when Icepick was approaching.

Walt acquired from a colleague who built high end guitar amplifiers with JBL speakers for Gibson, three military grade extended range handheld radios that operated on both UHF and VHF frequencies, with higher power outputs and upgraded antennas.

I heard the loud, deep throbbing exhaust of Icepick's motorcycle several minutes before I saw him pass by, and speaking tersely into the radio, I notified my confederates.

As soon as Icepick pulled up and dismounted, Jerry drove out from where he had been waiting in his pickup truck behind the house and sped off down the unpaved driveway.

Icepick got back on his bike and, with a flurry of gravel kicked up by the spinning rear wheel, chased after him.

Over the course of the next nine miles, Jerry and Icepick played a deadly game of cat-and-mouse.

Icepick was holding a sawed-off shotgun with one hand as he gripped the handlebars with the other. He accelerated whenever there was a straight section of road.

He had fired off two warning shots of twelve-gauge double-aught buckshot, but now the gun was empty, and he had no way to reload it while steering.

Jerry alternately swerved, hit the brakes, and floored the gas to impede Icepick from forcing him to comply, or shooting him.

Walt had furtively purloined from the Gibson factory where he worked in Nashville, a forty-foot coil of the Nickel wrapped steel wire, in B gauge, the company had developed in the 1950s and still used to string their specialty electric guitars.

He had taken the wire and strung it tightly between two trees on either side of the road.

He then let the wire go slack, so that it lay on the ground, where he carefully camouflaged it using leaves and dirt.

His intention was not to decapitate Icepick, but instead to cause a crash.

From Walt's hiding place, once he pulled the thin wire taught, it would be only a foot above the roadway and the impact would cause it to break.

He wrapped the wire several times loosely around the tree where he was hiding, so it would slide, and he could quickly deploy it.

When Jerry's truck came roaring down the road, with Icepick in hot pursuit on his Harley, Walt jerked the wire as soon as Jerry had passed, quickly twisting the wire to lock it in place.

At the last second, Icepick saw the wire spring up from the debris, but he had no time to react or avoid it.

The bike bucked and slid sideways as soon as the front wheel hit the wire, and Icepick was catapulted through the air.

When he landed, he rolled several times and abruptly came to a jarring halt with a loud thud against a sturdy tree.

Brandishing the dead deputy's pistol, Walt quickly emerged from his concealment at the side of the road, and without hesitation he delivered a *coup-de-grace*, shooting the disoriented and moaning Icepick in the head.

Then, he carefully removed the remaining wire from the trees, picked up the shotgun, and jogged up the road to where Jerry was waiting for him.

When the body was found, the ballistics from the slug in Icepick's cranium would match those on file for the deputy's gun.

CHAPTER TWENTY

Though at this point Jerry and I were completely unnerved, we were thankful Walt's plans had gone well.

But there remained one serious threat to our safety that needed urgent attention.

"Blue Eyes" Miller was an even more daunting adversary than Icepick had been.

We had read in the newspapers about his vicious reputation as a Dixie Mafia hit man, but, thankfully, none of us had ever met him.

Miller might not yet be aware of the disappearance of his *on-the-take* lawman, but he was sure to find out very soon about Icepick's murder.

Based on what Icepick had mentioned to Jerry, we knew that Miller had been maintaining a low profile since he had gone to ground in Tennessee, keeping his exact whereabouts and movements shrouded in secrecy.

Miller would be an elusive target, but Walt already had a plan in play to track him down.

Just as with Icepick's assassination, it was vital for Miller to die without any incriminating evidence that could be traced back to us.

The last thing any of us needed was to be arrested, or to become the focus of a relentless Dixie Mafia vendetta!

CHAPTER TWENTY-ONE

At Walt's suggestion, Jerry had reached out to a seedy nightclub owner, who he had become friendly with because the club promoted up and coming local musicians.

Jerry knew the place had a reputation for selling drugs and dubious cheap rotgut moonshine.

The proprietor was happy to accept a bribe when Jerry asked him to get word to Blue Eyes without identifying him.

He was to tell Miller that Icepick had suddenly split town and left behind a large stash of cocaine Jerry was nervous about, and anxious to get rid of.

Then, he would suggest a rendezvous that

evening at a secluded abandoned barn northwest of Columbia, so Jerry could give Miller the drugs.

The sizeable quantity of contraband at stake was sufficient to get Miller's immediate attention.

A few hours later, Jerry received a call confirming that Blue Eyes would be there, and we finalized our plans to ambush the gangster.

The location we had chosen was shunned by local inhabitants because it was on the outskirts of property owned by the Monsanto Chemical Company.

For decades, Monsanto had dumped and buried untold amounts of hazardous waste in the area, byproducts from their manufacture of toxic chemical warfare weapons.

Over the years, these corrosive contaminants had leaked out of buried barrels and tanks, polluting the groundwater, and poisoning the soil.

I was keeping watch when Miller arrived, and I radioed my compatriots informing them he was alone.

When Blue Eyes entered the ramshackle barn, Jerry motioned for him to inspect the drugs which were in a large duffle bag.

Blue Eyes approached him warily, with his pistol drawn, scanning from side-to-side looking for potential threats.

Walt was positioned above them over a light

fixture in the rafters and dropped down on Miller with Hartley's icepick in his outstretched hand, like an avenging angel or a bird of prey swooping in for the kill.

His attack was blurringly fast and he pinned Miller down as he knocked away the gun.

Then, he viciously stabbed Miller with the icepick up to the handle into one of the hoodlum's pale blue eyes.

As we stared at the dead man with the weapon impaled in his skull, we agreed that Miller dying as violently as all the victims he had mercilessly murdered was fitting retribution.

We threw the body into the trunk of Miller's Lincoln Continental, and I drove it to the parking lot of another one of the bars we knew paid protection to Icepick, which was closed for the night.

I left the motor running and made sure that no one saw me before hopping into Jerry's truck.

As we pulled out onto the road, Jerry and I breathed a collective sigh of relief.

Walt, the hardened veteran, seeming to take it all in stride, stared wordlessly out of the windshield with a stoic look.

But it occurred to me that the brutality of helping his friend must have awakened wartime memories best forgotten...

EPILOGUE

Kirksey McCord Nix, Jr., who was serving life in prison, had managed to continue and expand his criminal activities despite his incarceration.

His father, the Oklahoma judge, would pass away two years later.

But in the meantime, news of his son's alleged involvement from jail in setting up contract hits and extortion, continued to plague the judge and tarnish his good reputation.

When news of the murders of "Icepick" Hartley, and "Blue Eyes" Miller was reported to Nix Jr., he conferred with his jailed subordinates, and based on the police reports, they decided the missing

Cheatham County sheriff's deputy had betrayed them and was to blame.

This kind of infighting and disloyalty in the ranks wasn't good for business.

Nix quietly put the word out that he would pay $25,000 to whoever found and silenced the greedy cop...

Please enjoy the prologue of
Pirouette

PROLOGUE

The defense of Christendom during the crusades has often been romanticized in fiction.

More critical observers have pointed out that these wars were a political and imperialistic undertaking by the Catholic church.

For some who made the journey to the holy land, their motivation was primarily seen as an opportunity for personal glory and individual tests of martial prowess.

For others, however, taking up the cross was perceived as a pilgrimage in the service of God—an opportunity for salvation, and to prove worthiness for divine examination.

The Holy Roman Emperor Frederick I was one of the great European kings to answer the call to defend the holy land.

As a young knight, he fought beside his uncle, the German King Conrad III, on the Second Crusade.

Through the ensuing years, he gained a reputation as a fearsome warrior, charismatic leader, and clever strategist; due to his fiery temperament and red-colored beard, he was also known as Barbarossa in Italy and Kaiser Rotbart in Germany.

In 1189, after a longstanding political feud with Pope Urban III, King Frederick reconciled with the new Pope Gregory VIII.

He set off overland to return to the holy land and lend his considerable support on the Third Crusade at the head of a grand army.

His forces were to join those of the French King Philip II (known as Philip Augustus) and the English King Richard I (known as the Lionheart), who both traveled by sea.

En route to the holy land in June of 1190, King Frederick came to an untimely end in Turkey, when rather than wait to cross with his troops at a crowded bridge, he impatiently attempted to ford the Saleph River instead.

He and his majestic warhorse were swept away by the treacherous current, and weighed down by their heavy armor, they drowned.

Frederick's unexpected death left his troops leaderless and demoralized.

This, combined with continual attacks by Turkish forces led to devastating losses and desertions.

But some of Frederick's remaining army eventually made it to the holy land where they fought bravely in many great battles, including the famed siege of Acre.

One of the knights who persevered was Hermann Von Salza, who would go on to become the fourth Grand Master of The Order of Teutonic Knights, and confidant of the king—Holy Roman Emperor Frederick II.

Von Salza helped to lift that king's ex-communication of September 27th, 1227.

In Von Salza's entourage was a young penitent knight, who was seeking atonement for past sins...

ABOUT THE AUTHOR

E. Robert Brooks is an author and composer who writes historical fiction mystery stories featuring subjects such as:

Fine wine fraud- Wine Thief

Equestrian competition- Pirouette

Bicycle racing- Derailed Gears

Vintage motorcars- The Concours Caper

His published songs include:

Fire in the Heavens

Anathema Anthem

He is an amateur luthier, and has designed several custom guitars, including a version constructed of lightweight aerospace titanium.